To our four-legged friends everywhere,

The small and the tall
The shaggy and sleek
With huge hearts of gold
Each one unique!

Follow Silly Milly on Instagram @sillymillythedane

Also available in Milly's silly collection:

Printed in the United States of America
First Printing, 2019
ISBN: 978-1-7330943-1-3

A Silly Milly Christmas

Written by Sheri Wall

Illustrated by Ilona Sluijt · Designed by Erin Riddle

I have a *Great Dane* named *Milly*

She poses and primps willy-nilly!

Dressed fancy for guests

She wants to impress

Oh *Milly*, you make Christmas *silly*!

I have a *Great Dane* named *Milly*

She fogs up the glass *willy-nilly!*

Frozen at the window

Longing so for some snow

Oh *Milly*, you make Christmas *silly!*

I have a *Great Dane* named *Milly*

She waits for our friends willy-nilly!

From upstairs she can see

As they fill the entry

Oh *Milly*, you make Christmas *silly*!

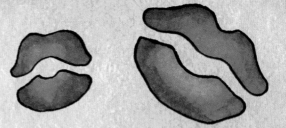

I have a Great Dane named Milly

She greets all the guests willy-nilly!

Mistletoe hanging high

Big dog kisses will fly

Oh Milly, you make Christmas silly!

I have a *Great Dane* named *Milly*

She samples the food willy-nilly!

With squares of french toast

And a bite of the roast

Oh *Milly*, you make Christmas *silly*!

I have a *Great Dane* named *Milly*

She decks all the halls willy-nilly!

Through branches of pine

She'll spy as we dine

Oh *Milly*, you make Christmas silly!

I have a *Great Dane* named *Milly*

She checks all the plates willy-nilly!

Dinner table works best

Heavy mug needs a rest

Oh *Milly*, you make Christmas *silly*!

I have a *Great Dane* named *Milly*
She begs for a snack willy-nilly!
She'll sit on command
For treats from my hand
Oh *Milly*, you make Christmas *silly*!

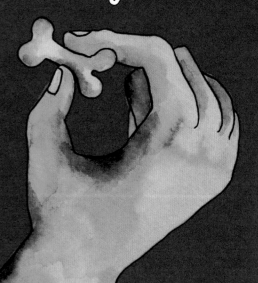

I have a *Great Dane* named *Milly*

She helps serve dessert willy-nilly!

Pushes bowl 'round the floor

'Til there's whipped cream no more

Oh *Milly*, you make Christmas silly!

I have a *Great Dane* named *Milly*

She licks and she laps willy-nilly!

Cool refreshment she stole

From the porcelain punch bowl

Oh *Milly*, you make Christmas silly!

I have a *Great Dane* named *Milly*

She unties the bows willy-nilly!

Digs through boxes and bags

'Cause she can't read the tags

Oh *Milly*, you make Christmas silly!

I have a *Great Dane* named *Milly*

She romps in the cold willy-nilly!

Small talk starts to bore

She darts out the back door

Oh *Milly,* you make Christmas *silly*!

I have a *Great Dane* named *Milly*
She sneaks through the house *willy-nilly!*
Is she naughty or nice
I don't have to think twice
Oh *Milly*, you make Christmas *silly!*

I have a *Great Dane* named *Milly*
She spreads joy and love willy-nilly!

Wishing holiday cheer

And a happy New Year

May your Christmas be so very *silly!*

Sheri Wall is a wife, mom, Great Dane aunt, Texan, and an award-winning children's book author. She uses rhymes and repetitive verse as essential learning tools in her writings. Sheri enjoys cooking, eating, decorating, bargain hunting, and being active. See more of Sheri's books at amatterofrhyme.com.

Ilona Stuijt is a traveling artist and illustrator from the Netherlands. She has worked on more than twenty books for children and adults. Ilona's paintings and illustrations are spread all over the globe. See Ilona's unique style at lankyartist.com.

Erin Riddle is a vintage-style photographer at Lone Star Pin-up and Vintage Luxe in Texas. In addition to loving Great Danes, she also enjoys singing, shopping, and entertaining friends and family. She is beyond excited to share a little holiday silliness with everyone through her lovable stinkmuffin, Milly.

Made in the USA
Monee, IL
28 November 2021